Rufus is a scruffy dog.
He is very good at handstands.

Gloria is a cockatoo.
She is a very good singer.

Neville is a frog.
He likes to dance.

Oscar is a sausage dog.
He loves skateboarding.

SIDNEY

The Little Blue Elephant

Sharon Rentta

ALISON
GREEN
BOOKS

This is Sidney.

He's quite little for an elephant.

These are Sidney's friends . . .

Oscar,

Rufus,

Gloria,

Neville

and Betty.

They're even smaller than Sidney.
They play together all the time.

But there are some games
that Sidney likes . . .

Watch out!
He's coming down!

Steady on, dude!

while his friends aren't so sure.

And there are some games
that his friends like,

Erm . . . You go on.
I'll catch you up.

but Sidney isn't keen at all.

Come on, Sidney! Let's have a race!

The fact was, Sidney had a secret.
He didn't know how to ride a bicycle!
Bicycles are tricky, especially for elephants.

He was worried his friends might laugh at him,
so he decided to have a go while they weren't looking.

He just had to find his balance . . .

. . . and work out how to steer.

How hard could it be?

Oh, dear.

Oof!

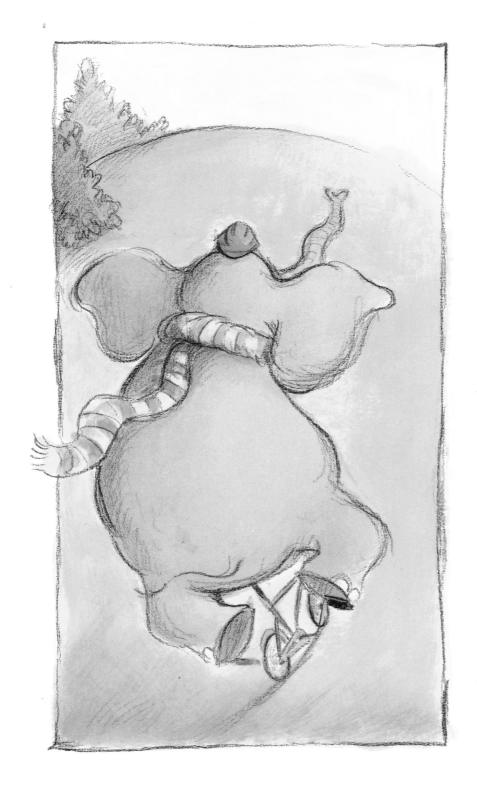

Oh . . .   Oh . . .

Oh, dear.

Meanwhile, Sidney's friends were having a lovely time.
But something was missing.
"I know!" shouted Rufus.

"Where's Sidney?"

They looked everywhere.

I think he was here.

I'm sure he was here.

He was definitely here.

But where was he now?

He went thataway!

"Poor Sidney!" said Oscar. "What happened?"

"Riding a bicycle is really hard," sighed Sidney.
"Especially for elephants."

"Never mind," said his friends. "We'll help you."

And off they set!

Sidney never even noticed when, one by one by one . . .

they all let go!

Am I really?

"Race you to the ice cream van!" said Sidney.
And guess who got there first?